Whuppity Stoorie

A SCOTTISH FOLKTALE

BY **CAROLYN WHITE**

ILLUSTRATED BY **S. D. SCHINDLER**

G. P. PUTNAM'S SONS • NEW YORK

Text copyright © 1997 by Carolyn White

Illustrations copyright © 1997 by S. D. Schindler

G. P. Putnam's Sons, a division of The Putnam & Grosset Group,

200 Madison Avenue, New York, NY 10016. G. P. Putnam's Sons,

Reg. U.S. Pat. & Tm. Off. Published simultaneously in Canada.

Printed in Hong Kong by South China Printing Co. (1988) Ltd.

Book designed by Donna Mark. Text set in Aurelia.

The art for this book was done with watercolors,

gouaches and pastels on colored mat board.

Library of Congress Cataloging-in-Publication Data

White, Carolyn, 1948– . Whuppity Stoorie/by Carolyn White;

illustrated by S. D. Schindler.   p.   cm.

Summary: When a fairy woman cures her pig, Kate's mother

has three days to guess the fairy's name or give Kate to her.

[1. Fairy tales.   2. Folklore—Scotland.]   I. Schindler, S. D., ill.

II. Title.   PZ8.W5775Wh   1997   398.2′09411′01—dc20

[E]   95-16-032   CIP   AC

ISBN 0-399-22903-5

1 3 5 7 9 10 8 6 4 2

First Impression

For my mom
C. W.

To Susan, Judy, Liz and Ruby,
my visual reference team
S. D. S.

n a cottage on a hilltop lived Kate of Kittlerumpit and her mother. They had little to eat and no fine clothes, but they had a handsome pig by the name of Grumphie, who was soon to farrow.

Every morning Kate filled Grumphie's trough with slops. Every day Kate tickled Grumphie behind the ears and told her stories. Every evening Kate played on her pipe Grumphie's favorite tune, *The Pigtown Fling*.

One morning Kate went to the sty to fill Grumphie's trough and found the pig on her back, squealing and groaning, her face white as soap.

"Mum," cried Kate, "come quick! Our Grumphie is sick."

Kate and her mother tried home remedies to make Grumphie well. They wrapped Grumphie in warm flannel. They fed her tea and toast. They tied red rowan berries around her neck to keep harm away. But Grumphie stayed sick, growing weaker and weaker. When Kate played *The Pigtown Fling*, Grumphie moaned.

Sadly, Kate's mother sat down on the knocking stone, Kate beside her. As the sun set, they wept for poor Grumphie, who wouldn't get well.

The Scots say that pigs see the wind, and that they hear what people cannot. Ill though she was, Grumphie lifted her head as if she heard or saw something strange. "What's that?" asked Kate, as a whirlwind, twirling dust and straw, rushed up the hill. From the wind's center, as calm as you please, stepped a lady in green, her face wrapped up in the hood of her mantle. She held a walking staff as tall as herself, and on her shoulder a sorrowful bird was sitting.

"Good woman of Kittlerumpit," said the green lady, "if I cure your pig, what will you give me?"

"Anything your ladyship asks," said the poor woman, dropping a curtsy. She knelt to kiss the hem of the green gown, but the green lady stopped her.

"None of your kissing and curtsying," said the green lady. "If you want your pig well, let's wet thumbs on the bargain."

Kate's mother and the green lady licked thumbs and stuck them together. Then the green lady marched into the sty. She stared at the sick pig and muttered what sounded to Kate and her mother like:

Pitter patter
Fairy water.

From out of her pouch she took a wee bottle and poured a green oil onto her fingers. No sooner had she rubbed oil on the pig's snout, behind the ears, and on the tip of the tail than Grumphie stood up and, with a grunt, strode to the trough for her supper.

Kate's mother was joyful. "What can I give you, good neighbor, for curing our Grumphie?"

"You'll not find me greedy," said the green lady. "All I ask, and *will* have, is your daughter."

The good woman of Kittlerumpit let out a howl because she knew now she had bargained with a fairy. She wept and she prayed, she begged and she scolded.

"Your screeching won't help you," said the fairy. "But one thing I'll tell you: I cannot—by fairy law—take your daughter until the third day from this day, and not then if you guess my name rightly."

Turning out of the pigsty, the green lady stepped back into the whirlwind and disappeared down the hill.

The good woman of Kittlerumpit didn't sleep that night nor the next night nor the next. When she wasn't hugging her daughter and crying her heart out, she was rapidly reading a big book of names.

"Maybe *Jean* is the green lady's name," said the mother. "Or maybe it's *Margaret*. Or *Mairi*. Or *Isabel*. Or *Agnes*." She turned page after page, so caught up in her reading that she didn't see Grumphie steal out of her sty and run down the hill.

"Grumphie, come back here," cried Kate, chasing after her pig. Grumphie wouldn't listen. She ran through a forest. She swam across a stream. Kate followed as Grumphie climbed down into an old quarry hole grown over with gorse, a bonny spring in the center.

Kate heard the whirring of a wheel and a voice singing. So she hid behind a bush, Grumphie beside her, and saw the green woman working hard at a spinning wheel, spinning a green dress like her own, only smaller.

"Corbie," said the green lady to the bird on her shoulder, "do you think the girl Kate will look good in fairy green?"

"Caw," answered the bird. The green woman cackled. The spinning wheel turned faster and faster, creating a great wind. Up jumped the green lady, and she began twirling and dancing, a wicked joy in her heart. Around her the bird flew as she sang:

At sunset tonight the girl I'll claim,
Sure as Whuppity Stoorie *is my name.*

"Ssh! Grumphie," Kate whispered, "let's go home and tell Mum the wild fairy's name." Slowly the girl and the pig crept out of the quarry. Fast they swam across the stream. Fast they ran through the forest. But a whirlwind crying "Whuppity! Whuppity!" spun past them and rushed ahead up the hill.

Kate's mother was sitting on the knocking stone, reading mightily, when the whirlwind appeared, and the green lady stepped sprightly out of the center.

"Good woman of Kittlerumpit," said the fairy, "well you know what I come for. Stand and deliver the girl."

"Not if your name is *Storm O'Dust*," said Kate's mother.

The green lady chuckled. Even the bird laughed.

"What about *Green Skirt*?" continued the mother. "Or *Windy Woman*? Or *Sunset Whirl*?"

"The girl's mine," said the green lady.

"Maybe your name's *Mayblossom*. Or *Chamomile*. Or *Thistle*. Or *Fuchsia*."

"I've not got all day," said the impatient fairy.

"What about *Lily Crocodilly*? Or *Fiddletot*? Or *Reedledeedee*?"

"Give the girl here," said the green lady.

"Good neighbor," pleaded the mother, "leave my daughter and take me."

"Are you daft?" scoffed the fairy. "Your daughter's the bargain. It's your daughter I'll have."

"No one takes my daughter from me," said the good woman of Kittlerumpit, clenching her fist.

"Mum," cried Kate, running up the hill, "where are the good manners you taught me? That's no way to greet the high and mighty princess *Whuppity Stoorie*."

The fairy leaped into the air, landing hard on her shoe heels. Then down the hill she whirled, screeching with rage.

Kate and her mother joined hands and danced, singing:

Whuppity Haw! Whuppity Hey!
Whuppity Stoorie *is her name.*

"Where's Grumphie?" asked Kate's mother.

"She was with me in the forest," said Kate.

"Whuppity Stoorie better not harm a bristle on Grumphie's snout," said her mother.

Down the hill mother and daughter ran until they found Grumphie in the dirt, three baby pigs at her breast.

Now every morning Kate filled the trough with enough slops to feed Grumphie and Curlie-Tail, Guffey and Jig. Every day Kate tickled Grumphie and her babies behind their ears and told them the story of Whuppity Stoorie. And every evening when Kate played her pipe, the four pigs of Kittlerumpit grunted to the tune of *The Pigtown Fling*.